Jasper
and the Bully

Story by Michèle Dufresne
Illustrations by Sterling Lamet

Jasper and the Bully
ISBN 978-1-58453-234-7
ISBN 978-1-58453-232-3 (Set of Two Titles)
Written by Michèle Dufresne
Illustrated by Sterling Lamet

Printed in the United States of America.

10 9 8 7 6

Contents

Chapter 1: Home from School   2

Chapter 2: Jack the Bully   10

Chapter 3: Jasper Goes to School   17

Chapter 4: Scare the Bully   23

Chapter 5: A Goblin and a Ghost   26

Chapter 6: Following Sweet Face   37

Chapter 7: Homework Help   54

Chapter 1

Home from School

Jasper likes to sleep in the front yard in the afternoon, so he can watch for Katie coming home from school.

One beautiful spring day, Sweet Face was chasing a moth. There was a pleasant humming sound coming from bumblebees in a nearby bush.

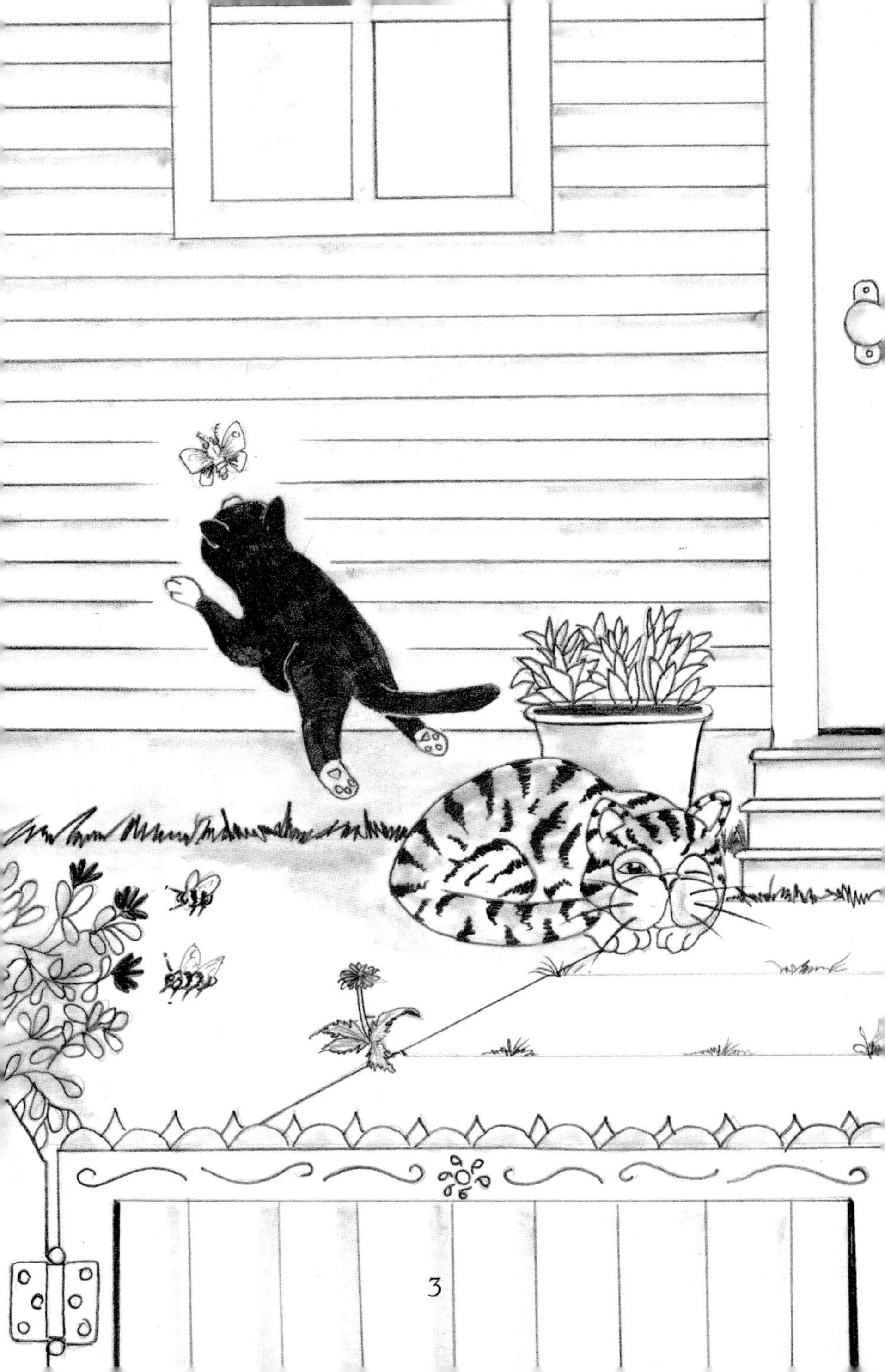

Jasper's ears perked up. He could hear Katie coming down the walk. He got up and stretched, because the first thing Katie did when she came through the gate was to pick up Jasper and scratch his ears and kiss his nose. Jasper pretended not to like this. He would wiggle in Katie's arms and pretend that he wanted to get away, but secretly he looked forward to the kisses.

Today, Katie walked by Jasper without even saying hello. The pink hair ribbons that Katie had been wearing when she left for school in the morning were missing.

Katie's face was smudged with dirt, and it looked like she had been crying.

Jasper followed Katie into the house. She dropped her backpack onto the kitchen table with a bang.

Ms. Gomez, Katie's mother, was unpacking a bag of groceries.
"Hi, Katie," she said as she emptied the bag. "How was school?"

Jasper trotted over to sniff a grocery bag on the floor. Something in the bag smelled good.

Ms. Gomez stepped around Jasper as she opened the refrigerator door. She was still dressed in her work clothes — a skirt and silky blouse, and shoes with sharp, pointed heels that always made Jasper nervous.

Katie didn't answer. She stared down at the table and chewed her lip.

Katie's mother turned around to look at Katie. "Katie! What happened to you? Oh, dear! Sweetie, you've been crying, haven't you? What happened?"

"Nothing," sniffled Katie. "Nothing happened." She wiped her eyes.

"Katie, something has happened!" Katie's mother got a dish towel and wet it at the sink. Then she began to wash Katie's face. "Are you hurt?" she asked.

"I just fell," said Katie. "I'm fine."

Katie took the towel from her mother's hands and finished wiping her face. Then she grabbed an apple from the bowl on the counter. "I'm going upstairs to do my homework." She picked up her backpack and headed for the stairs.

"Are you sure you're all right?" asked her mother. She looked worried.

"I'm sure. I'm really fine!" Katie replied.

Jasper followed Katie up the stairs.
Katie sat down on her bed. Her eyes
were wet, and she kept sniffling.

Jasper jumped on the bed and
snuggled up to Katie.

Katie patted Jasper but didn't kiss
him or scratch his ears. Something was
definitely wrong!

Chapter 2

Jack the Bully

After dinner, Jasper followed Katie over to Tony's house. Tony was sitting on a tire swing tied in the backyard.

Katie climbed onto the tire swing with Tony. Jasper lay down nearby. Scruffy, Tony's dog, ran up to Jasper and wagged his tail to play, but Jasper ignored the dog.

"Did you tell your mom?" asked Tony.

Jasper's ears perked up. Tell Mom what?

"No," answered Katie. "I didn't tell her."

"How come you didn't tell her? She could do something!" said Tony.

"Remember when Jack was teasing Teddy Carter a couple of months ago? And Teddy's mom called the teacher and the principal? Remember what happened?"

"Oh, yeah," said Tony.

The two children were silent while they remembered what happened to Teddy when he told on Jack — the teasing got worse. Jack never seemed to get caught by any adult.

"I think it's better to put up with it. He'll get bored and move on to bullying someone else," Katie told Tony.

Jack the bully! Jasper knew all about him. He was a big, mean boy who loved to take other kids' lunch money and push smaller kids around. No one wanted to be friends with Jack.

Jasper's tail twitched. Jasper did not like to see Katie so unhappy.

"He shouldn't get away with all his mean bullying," said Tony.

"No he shouldn't!" said Katie. "He doesn't fight fair. But thanks for sharing your lunch with me."

"I know he took your lunch money, but did anything else happen?" Tony asked Katie.

"He followed me home and kept pushing me," said Katie. "He pulled my hair, and it really hurt. He took my hair ribbons. Then I tripped on the sidewalk and fell down. Jack laughed and ran off."

"We need to do something about Jack," said Tony.

Jasper was thinking the same thing. But what could be done?

Chapter 3

Jasper Goes to School

The next afternoon, instead of waiting in the yard for Katie to come home from school, Jasper climbed over the fence and went down the sidewalk toward the school. He heard something behind him. He turned and looked. It was Sweet Face. Jasper hissed at the little cat.

Sweet Face tipped her head and twitched her tail.

Ever since Sweet Face had come to live with the family, she had followed Jasper around wherever he went.

Jasper decided to ignore Sweet Face. He turned back around and continued to trot down the sidewalk, until he came to a large oak tree near the school. He scrambled up the tree and found a comfortable lookout spot facing the school.

The leaves on the tree started to rustle and the branch Jasper was sitting on began to sway. It was Sweet Face, joining him in the tree. Jasper sighed. Why did Sweet Face have to do everything he did?

"Meow!" said Sweet Face. "Meow!"

Jasper looked at the little black cat. She snuggled up next to him. How annoying! He made a soft, warning growl from deep in his throat, but Sweet Face didn't move away.

The door of the school opened and children began pouring out of the school. Some of the children climbed onto waiting school buses, while others got into cars parked along the curb. Where was Katie?

Jasper watched and waited. Finally, when the last bus and car had pulled away, he could see Katie coming. She walked slowly and looked all around. When she got to the sidewalk, she picked up speed and began jogging toward home. Jasper was about to jump down and follow her when he saw a large boy jump out of some bushes near the tree.

"Oh, Katie," said the boy. "Where are you going so fast? Did you forget something?"

Jasper recognized him. It was Jack the bully.

Katie turned around slowly. Jasper could see that Katie was afraid.

"I don't have any money today to give you," she said to Jack. "My mom didn't give me any lunch money. She made my lunch. I have some left, though. You can have it."

"I don't want your leftover lunch," said Jack. "I told you, I want your money!"

"I'll bring it tomorrow," said Katie.

"You'd better," threatened Jack. "Or else!"

Chapter 4

Scare the Bully

Tony came over to Katie's after dinner so they could work on their homework together. Jasper and Sweet Face sat on Katie's bed and watched.

"I wish I didn't have soccer practice after school," said Tony. "Jack wouldn't bother you if the two of us were walking together."

"I need to think of something," said Katie. "I feel so angry and upset! Today I asked Mom for a bag lunch, thinking that if I didn't have any money, Jack would leave me alone. But no such luck."

"I think you should tell your teacher or the principal. Or at least tell your mom," said Tony.

Katie groaned. "I know that would only make it worse. The trouble is that if I keep giving him money, he will never leave me alone."

"You know," said Tony, "most bullies really are scared inside."

"I don't think Jack is scared of anything," Katie said to Tony.

"Something must scare him," said Tony.

"Yeah, but what?"

The two children went back to their homework, but Jasper kept thinking. How could he scare the bully?

Chapter 5

A Goblin and a Ghost

Katie and her mother were eating breakfast. Ms. Gomez turned around and saw Jasper dragging something into the kitchen. "What's Jasper got there?" she asked Katie.

"It's the Halloween costume I made him last year," said Katie. "You know, the goblin costume."

"I thought he hated that costume," said Katie's mother.

Katie giggled. "I know. But look!
I think he wants me to put it on him."

"That's very strange," said her mother.

Katie reached down and picked up
the goblin costume. Jasper looked up at
Katie.

"You know, I was joking, but I really do think he wants me to put it on him," said Katie. "Maybe he wants to play 'dress up' today while I'm at school. I'll get Sweet Face's ghost costume, too. They can both dress up."

Katie ran to her room and returned with Sweet Face's ghost costume. She put the goblin costume on Jasper and the ghost costume on Sweet Face. "You cute things," she said. "Have fun while I'm at school!"

Jasper looked at Sweet Face. What was Sweet Face doing in that ghost costume? Jasper hissed at her.

Sweet Face gave a sweet "Meow" and
lay down. Jasper lay down too. It was
going to be a long day, hanging around
in these stupid costumes, but that's how
it had to be.

The day crawled by. Finally, Jasper
heard a car pull into the driveway.

Ms. Gomez came into the house
and saw the two cats in their Halloween
costumes.

"Oh, you poor things," said Ms. Gomez. "Have you been in those costumes all day?" She reached down, but Jasper slipped by her and dashed out the open door. Sweet Face followed right behind.

Jasper ran up the street. He hoped Sweet Face wouldn't ruin things. When he got to the same tree he had been in the day before, he climbed up to the big branch and settled down to wait.

Sweet Face followed him to the tree and climbed up, too. She sat down right beside him. Jasper looked over at the little cat. She looked very strange in her ghost costume!

Soon children were streaming out of the school. Katie didn't wait until everyone was gone, as she had done the day before. Today, she dashed out of the school right away and started down the sidewalk.

Jasper could see the bushes below, where Jack was hiding. As soon as Jack jumped out, Jasper let out a loud yowl. He launched himself at the bully, landing right on top of Jack.

Jack felt a sharp pain. He gasped and turned to look at his shoulder.

Jack stared at the strange orange creature with huge teeth clawing his shoulder and hissing at him. His eyes grew bigger and bigger as he gulped and started to scream. "Help! Help! Get this thing off me!" He ran around in a panic, trying to get the creature off him.

All of a sudden, Tony and the other kids on the soccer team came around the corner of the school. They had come to help Katie. When they saw Jack screaming and running around in a circle, they stopped and stared at the sight.

Thump! A second white object flew out of nowhere and landed on top of Jack's head, hissing and spitting. White cloth flapped over Jack's eyes.

Now Jack couldn't see anything.
"Ahhh!" he screeched. "Ahhh! Get off of
me!"

Tony turned to the other kids and
laughed. "Look! It's Jasper and Sweet
Face, Katie's cats!"

"Keep your mean cats away from me!"
shouted Jack the bully.

"Scaredy cat, scaredy cat!" sang one of the girls Jack used to torment. "Jack is a scaredy cat, afraid of kitty cats!"

"They aren't cats!" said Jack, sputtering with anger. "They're demons!"

Katie walked over and plucked Sweet Face off of Jack's head. Jasper jumped to the ground.

She pulled the goblin costume off of Jasper and the ghost costume off of Sweet Face. Jasper shook himself and sniffed.

"Sure," said Katie. "I'll take them home. But you had better stay away from me." She grinned over at Tony.

Tony shook his head and laughed. "Come on," he said to the other kids on the soccer team. "It turns out we can have practice after all!" He waved to Katie and turned toward the soccer field. Katie tucked Sweet Face under her arm and leaned over to scratch Jasper's ear.

"You are the best cat," she whispered in Jasper's ear.

Jasper trotted off behind Katie, following her home. Of course he was the best cat! He knew that already.

Chapter 6

Following Sweet Face

Sweet Face peeked out at Jasper from under Katie's arm. She had a funny look on her face. What was the little cat's problem now? She had done a good job helping him scare the bully. She should look more pleased with herself!

Katie ran into the kitchen as soon as they got home. She threw down her backpack on the floor and began to dance around. "Mom! You should have seen Jasper and Sweet Face today. They were amazing!"

When Katie finished telling her mother the whole story, Ms. Gomez didn't say anything for a few minutes. Then she spoke. "Katie, you should have told me about this before."

"But Mom, you couldn't have helped," said Katie.

"Yes, I could have. It is my job to make sure you're safe. Katie, I am the grownup. It's not okay for you to keep something like this from me."

Jasper sat next to his bowl, hoping all the serious stuff would end and someone would get his dinner. Sweet Face began to scratch at the door to go out.

Where did she think she was going?
Jasper was puzzled.

Katie opened the door for Sweet Face. Sweet Face ran out and Jasper went out behind her. Where was she going? Jasper followed her out through the gate and up the street.

As they came around the corner, Jasper saw the nasty bully, Jack. He was walking very slowly, kicking at rocks on the sidewalk. Jasper was surprised to see Jack's eyes looking red. There were smudges of dirt on his face, as if he had been wiping away tears with a dirty hand. Jack, crying?

Sweet Face followed Jack, and Jasper
followed Sweet Face.

Jack stopped at a small house and sat
down on the front steps. Sweet Face sat
down near a bush in the yard, and Jasper
joined her. All of a sudden, Sweet Face
got up and walked toward Jack. Jasper
watched anxiously. What was Sweet Face
doing?

When Sweet Face got close to Jack, she sat down and began meowing in a very sad, pitiful voice.

Jack looked up. "Hey!" he said. "You're one of those mean cats of Katie's."

"Meow," said Sweet Face. "Meow."

Jack looked nervous. He slid to the back of the steps, holding his backpack in front of him for protection.

"Meow," said Sweet Face. "Meow." She lay down in the grass looking pitiful.

Sweet Face peeked back at Jasper, who sat watching all this from behind a bush.

"Ummm, are you lost?" Jack asked.

"Meow," said Sweet Face. "Meow."

"Go home!" said Jack. "Go home. I'm not going to do anything again to Katie!"

"Meow," said Sweet Face. "Meow." She tipped her head and looked at Jack.

"Go home," said Jack again.

"Meow," said Sweet Face. "Meow."

"Oh, boy," said Jack. "What am I supposed to do? Well, stay there if you want to. See if I care!" He picked up his backpack and opened a zippered pocket, pulling out a key. He got up and unlocked the door. With one last look at Sweet Face, Jack went into the house.

Sweet Face didn't move. She lay in the grass. The sun went down and it was getting dark. Jasper wasn't sure what to do.

"Meow!" he said from the bush. He started toward Sweet Face, but she hissed at him.

Sweet Face never hissed at him!
Jasper was stunned. He sat down. What
was the little cat doing?

Then the door of the house opened
and Jack looked out. Sweet Face was still
lying in the grass.

"Meow," said Sweet Face. "Meow."

"Why are you still here?" Jack asked
Sweet Face. "Go home!"

45

"Meow," said Sweet Face. "Meow."

"All right," announced Jack. "I will take you home. You can't sit here all night!"

He closed the door of the house and locked it. Then he marched over to Sweet Face and picked her up. Sweet Face snuggled into the boy's arms and began purring.

Jasper was amazed. Sweet Face was acting like Jack was a special friend. Why? What was she doing?

Jack turned and began walking toward Katie's house. Jasper followed along at a distance, trying to keep out of sight.

"Nice kitty," Jasper heard Jack say to Sweet Face. He could hear Sweet Face purring.

When they got to the house, Katie was in the yard with her mother, calling for Jasper and Sweet Face. When she saw Sweet Face in Jack's arms, she ran to the gate. "What are you doing to my cat?"

"Nothing," said Jack. "Just bringing her back to you. She followed me home."

"Do you have Jasper, too?" Katie asked. Just then, Jasper darted out of the shadows and ran into the house.

"Mom, this is Jack Howard, the boy I told you about," said Katie.

"I know Jack," said Ms. Gomez. "Jack, do you remember me? I was your preschool teacher when you were four. Come inside for a minute. I'd like to talk to you."

"Um, I should be getting h-h-home," stuttered Jack.

"It won't take long," said Katie's mother.

Jack went into the house and followed Ms. Gomez into the kitchen. Katie's math book and papers were spread out on the table. Pots were boiling on the stove.

They all sat down at the kitchen table.
"Jack, Katie tells me you have been
asking her for her lunch money and
doing a lot of teasing," said Ms. Gomez.

Jack was very quiet. He looked down
at his hands.

"How would you feel if someone did
this to you?"

"Um, pretty bad, I guess," said Jack.
He looked embarrassed.

"You need to think about how you would feel if you were the one being teased," said Katie's mother. "You need to put yourself in the other person's shoes. Do you understand what I'm saying?"

Jack thought for a minute. "I think so," he told Ms. Gomez.

Jasper listened. Of course Jack wasn't going to do anything more ever again to Katie! If he did, he would have Jasper to deal with!

Now that the problem was settled, Jasper began to think about his dinner. Wasn't it time to eat?

Sweet Face looked over at Jasper. Then she marched over to Jack and rubbed against the boy's leg. "Meow!" she said.

Katie laughed. "Sweet Face seems to like you, Jack," she told him.

Jack leaned over to pet Sweet Face. Sweet Face purred.

"You think so?" asked Jack.

Sweet Face jumped up onto Jack's lap.

"Oh, yes," said Katie.

"Well, if we have everything cleared up here, I have some homemade chocolate chip cookies for anyone who is hungry," Ms. Gomez said. "I know it's close to dinner time, but I think it would be all right, just this once."

"Does your mother know you're here?" Katie's mother asked Jack. "It's getting pretty dark. Maybe I should drive you home after you have a cookie."

Jasper's tail twitched. Chocolate chip cookies! Would there be any for him?

Chapter 7

Homework Help

The next day, Katie and Tony headed off to school. Jasper could hear them talking about Jack.

"So, let me get this straight," said Tony. "He brought Sweet Face home, your mom gave him chocolate chip cookies, and then he helped you with your math homework?"

"Yup," said Katie. "Plus, Sweet Face adores him. She kept purring and purring."

"I guess you never know," said Tony.
"He seemed to be just a bully. But now it
looks like he was just trying to get
attention. I guess your cats helped with
that!"

"So you don't think there will be any more trouble from Jack, then?" asked Tony.

"No," replied Katie. "Thanks to Jasper and Sweet Face."

Tony and Katie turned the corner, and Jasper could no longer hear their voices. Tony was right — you never know! Sweet Face had somehow decided that Jack was worth helping. Jasper couldn't figure out how she knew, but she did.

Jasper looked at the little cat sitting under a tree, watching a bird making a nest. What had made her follow that boy? Why did she get him to bring her home?

Jasper yawned. Enough thinking. It
was time for a nap!

JASPER THE CAT
CHAPTER BOOKS FOR INDEPENDENT READERS

Jasper and the Bully

Sweet Face's Adventure

Word Count

Chapter 1: 432
Chapter 2: 310
Chapter 3: 389
Chapter 4: 180
Chapter 5: 753
Chapter 6: 1165
Chapter 7: 198